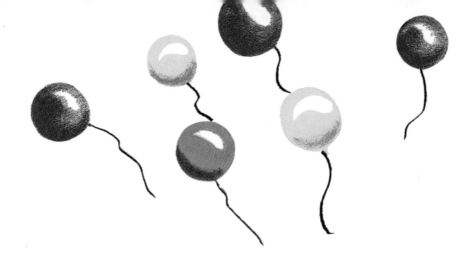

First Chronicle Books edition published in 2005.

Original jacket design and hand-lettered type by Clement Hurd.
Type design by Mary Beth Fiorentino.
Typeset in Futura.
Manufactured in China.

Library of Congress Cataloging-in-Publication Data
Hurd, Clement, 1908-1988.
        The merry chase / written and illustrated by Clement Hurd.– 1st
Chronicle Books ed.
        p. cm.
Summary: Upon meeting a dog at a street corner, a cat runs as fast as she can
and leads him on a merry chase through kitchens, across tables, over people,
and under traffic until finally reaching a safe haven.
        ISBN 0-8118-4967-8
        1. Cats–Juvenile fiction. 2. Dogs–Juvenile fiction. [1. Cats–Fiction. 2.
Dogs–Fiction.] I. Title.
PZ10.3.H963Me 2005
[E]–dc22
        2004021582

Distributed in Canada by Raincoast Books
9050 Shaughnessy Street, Vancouver, British Columbia V6P 6E5

10 9 8 7 6 5 4 3 2 1

Chronicle Books LLC
85 Second Street, San Francisco, California 94105

www.chroniclekids.com

THE
MERRY
CHASE

Written and Illustrated by
CLEMENT HURD

chronicle books · san francisco

One day a man was taking his Dog for a walk.
Around the corner came a lady with her Cat.

"Meow," said the Cat.

"Woof!" said the Dog.

And then the merry chase began.

Snap! the Dog broke his leash.

Whee! the Cat got away.

"Bow wow,"

barked the Dog and knocked over the ladder.

The Cat ran as fast as she could.

The Dog came around the corner

as the Cat went in through an open door.

The Cat jumped over the kitchen table and

spilled the soup. The Dog went under the table.

"Yippee," barked the Dog

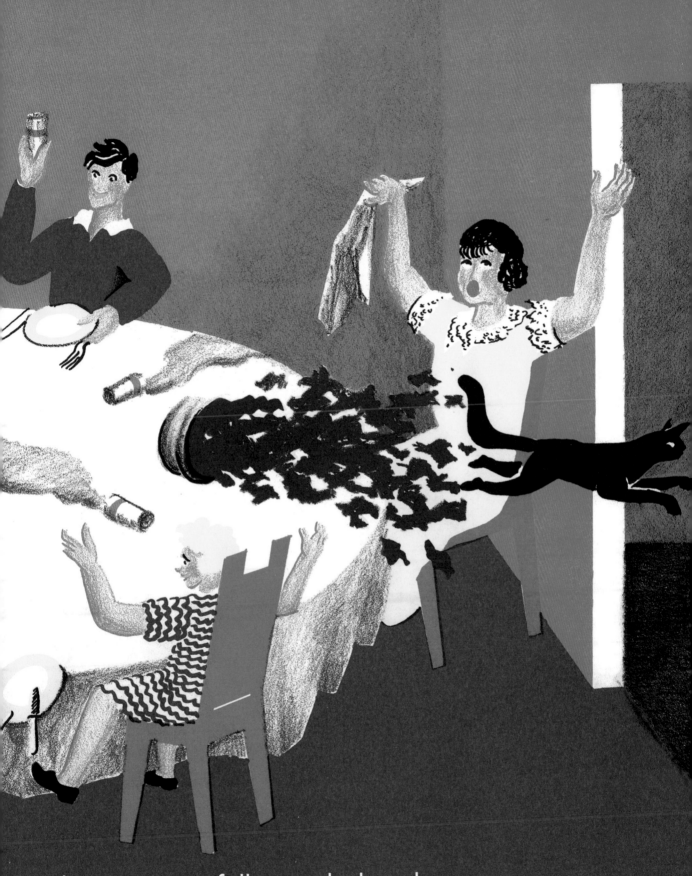

as the Cat went full speed ahead.

The Dog jumped over the sofa and landed

on the man's stomach. The Cat ran on

The Cat jumped out of the window,

the nurse fell over the chair. The Dog lost his way.

"Bow wow,"
barked the Dog and the painter

fell off his stand. The Cat ran inside.

The Dog was going so fast that the Cat

went right through the baker's window.

The Dog leaped out of the window as the Cat

upset the applecart and ran into a butcher shop.

The Cat jumped up on the butcher's hat.
The Dog couldn't reach her. The man
was very glad to find his Dog and the
lady to find her Cat. Then the butcher
gave the Dog a bone and the Cat a fish

and that was the end of the merry chase.